The Wonderful Story of

Melody Yodel

Written & Illustrated By:

MC WINGSTEDT

AuthorHouse™
1663 Liberty Drive
Bloomington, IN 47403
www.authorhouse.com
Phone: 1 (800) 839-8640

Published by AuthorHouse 05/23/2017

ISBN: 978-1-5246-8706-9 (sc)
ISBN: 978-1-5246-8707-6 (e)

Library of Congress Control Number: 2017908166

Print information available on the last page.

authorHOUSE®

The Wonderful Story of
Melody Yodel

You say that you can't find your best teddy bear?
It's not in your room?
It's not anywhere?
Perhaps you will find it before all is said.
Not now, though, my darling. It's now time for bed.

But I'll tell you a story.
It may help you right now,
when you feel a bit lost,
and you're frowning your brow.

Let me sit down beside you.
Let dream pictures guide you.
You'll see then
what I have to tell.

Miss Melody Yodel
was an old lady who
had a penchant for
wearing strange hats.

She had hats that had feathers,
a hat with a bell.
She had large hats with streamers,
and small hats to tell
of her great admiration for caps that adorn.
(I heard that she once had a hat with a horn!)

Miss Melody had a fine hat for each day;
for every occasion... for every school play;
for every night out, and for every foray.
Miss Melody loved her fine hats.

Then one sunny day, Miss Melody Yodel
stood very far back from her loaded hat rack
and exclaimed:
"I need more room!"

So she gathered her sweaters, her treasures and trim,
and she packed up her hat pack--
right up to the brim.
And she started to walk into town.

She dreamed of a big house
with rooms for each hat
and of spaces for feathers and down.

She continued her dreams
as the first raindrops fell.
When the sky became dark
church bells started to knell.
Then the wind whipped around
in a mad angry spell
and Miss Melody Yodel
stumbled and fell.

Her glorious hats
tumbled out of her pack.
And, as if they had wings,
they flew up, down and back —
and were gone.

Now Melody Yodel—poor little old lady—
had lost both her hats and her dreams.
She sat at the edge of a bench nearby.
She was chilled to the bone,
too unhappy to cry.

The rain started to stop.
The wind stopped with a start
The clouds drew apart, and Melody Yodel
looked into her heart.

Then she smiled.

She had heard a small sound.
So she looked all around
for that sweet tiny sound
somewhere down near the ground.

Then she saw it.
Right near where she sat
stood the lovely wet form
of a very small cat.
For the second time
on this bad afternoon
Miss Melody started to grin.

Then she leaned over
to pick up the cat.

As she reached out to lift him
the cat took a leap,
surprisingly, landing
on all his four feet
smack on the top of her head!

"Oh gracious!" Miss Melody
shouted out loud.
And she did a strange dance
that gathered a crowd.

"Look at that!" someone said,
"What a wonderful hat!
Miss Yodel, it looks like
You're wearing a cat!"

And she was.

The little cat blinked
and puffed up his fine tail
'til it shielded Miss Melody's eyes
Like a veil.

"Well," Melody thought.
"There's some good in that.
Have you any more tricks
you lost little cat?"

And he did.

The little cat smiled
as he waved his broad tail
like a flag in the air.
What panache! What a flare!

Such a beautiful hat!
What a talented cat!
He'll assume any pose, change his style,
just like that!

Miss Yodel remembered
her ribbons and strings,
her bangles and do-dads,
her beads and her rings.

And she thought,
"For all that,
I think I would rather
Have one special hat."

So she said to the cat,
"How's this for a deal?
Each day I will give you
a fine tasty meal
and a warm comfy bed...

"You have only to
ride on my head as I go.
At times you might carry a rose —
just for show."

"What say you, dear fine cat,
'Yes' or 'no'?"

The cat snuggled down
in Miss Melody's curls
and he sleepily batted
at Melody's pearls.

Then he slept.

"So, you want me to guess?"
she said to the cat.
I'm taking all this
for a 'Yes..'"

And so it began.

Now wherever Miss Melody Yodel may go,
she carries along her fine cat-hat, "Shapp-O."

If she's driving along or just walking about,
she is never alone.
She is never without
her beautiful, talented, stylish Shapp-O.

Shapp-O loves his life;
and he's really quite clever,
assuming fine poses and
waving a feather.

And that's that.

I guess what this tells you
is something that's bad
may turn out in the end
to be happy, not sad.

And so if you ever are caught in the rain,
look around for your cat/hat....
Quit crying in vain.
Stick it out. Wait around.
Hang on tight to this ride,
(and who knows?)
what you need may be right at your side.

CPSIA information can be obtained
at www.ICGtesting.com
Printed in the USA
LVOW06s0002290817
546737LV00020B/233/P